Snowdrifts

Story by Oliver Postgate
Pictures by Peter Firmin

Severnside Books

Snow was falling in the top left-hand
corner of Wales. Flakes the size of old pennies
floated gently from the dark grey sky and laid
themselves carefully on the ground.

There was so much of it!

The little town of Llaniog, high in the hills, was quite covered.

The roads were blocked.

The railway was blocked.

People dug paths from door to door but the snow soon covered them again.

2

Ivor the Engine was snug and warm in his shed on the siding. So were the sheep who had come down off the hill to warm themselves by his boiler. In fact, there were sheep everywhere in the town. They huddled in the High Street and clustered around Eli the Baker's shop, where the smell of new-baked bread floated out among the snowflakes.

Eli the Baker was a very worried man. The storeroom where he kept his flour was usually full to the ceiling with flour bags, but now it was empty. He had used up all the flour. He put on his overcoat and scarf and tramped out into the snow.

On the way he met Mr Davies the Grocer and Mrs Williams the Sweetshop.

"What are you out of then?" asked Eli.

"Everything," replied Mr Davies. "Rice, treacle, butter, jam, biscuits, potatoes. You name it, I haven't got it. My shop is almost empty!".

"So is mine," sighed Mrs Williams.

Dai Station the Station-master and Jones the Steam the engine driver, sat in the booking office at Llaniog Station with their feet up on the stove, drinking tea.

There came a knock at the door. It opened and in came a lot of cold air, some snowflakes, Eli the Baker, Mr Davies and Mrs Williams.

"What's this?" asked Dai Station. "There are no tickets or trains today."

"No flour," said Eli.

"No potatoes," said Mr Davies.

"No bull's-eyes," said Mrs Williams.

"Oh yes," said Dai Station, "what are you going to do about that then?"

"There's nothing we can do," growled Eli. "The flour is waiting at Grumbly Town for Ivor to collect as usual. Until it comes we shan't have any more bread."

"Or potatoes," said Mr Davies.

"Or jelly-babies," said Mrs Williams.

"Oh, there's tragedy now," said Jones. "What shall we eat?"

"We shan't eat, we shall starve," explained Eli the Baker, "unless you and Ivor go to Grumbly and collect the goods."

"But the snow is deep on the line," said Jones the Steam. "We would never get through without a snowplough!"

"Then get a snowplough," said Eli the Baker firmly and went home.

Well, of course, Eli the Baker was quite right. The only thing to do was to get a snowplough.

Jones the Steam and Dai Station took their feet off the stove, finished their tea and went to see Beynon the Smith.

"Snowploughs is it?" said Beynon Smith thoughtfully. "I've no idea what snowploughs look like, so I suppose I shall just have to invent one. It would be a sort of double sideways shovel, I expect. Something like this perhaps..."

Beynon Smith took a piece of burnt wood from the forge and drew on the wall.

"A bolt here at the back, look, and a bracket over Ivor's buffers of two-inch angle, riveted plates..."

Once Beynon Smith is busy inventing something, there is no point in standing about. He was still drawing and talking to himself as Jones and Dai walked back to the station. Jones the Steam went on down to the shed to see to Ivor's fire and tell him about the snowplough.

Beynon Smith did not waste time. He hammered and thumped and welded sheet and angles and bars of steel in his forge, and by midday he was to be seen dragging a strange implement over the snow like a sledge.

He bolted it to Ivor's front end, over the buffers. It fitted very well.

"Go on Ivor!" said Beynon. "Take a run at the snow!"

Jones the Steam opened Ivor's regulator as wide as it would go and Ivor fairly charged at the deep snow. The snowplough dug its point in and threw the snow up each side of the line in a great shower.

"Keep going, Ivor!" shouted Beynon Smith as he jumped on to the step.

Ivor kept going and carved a clean path through the snow up to Llaniog Station.

There they coupled up two trucks and were ready to go to Grumbly.

"Shall we try it then, Ivor?" asked Jones.

POOP-POOP! went Ivor's whistle.

CHUFF CHUFF CHUFF went Ivor's pistons.

SCRUNCH...ER...SLURP...went the snow as it was hoisted up and thrown aside by the snowplough.

"Keep pushing, Ivor!" shouted Beynon Smith and Dai Station as they disappeared down the line.

The snowdrifts lay thick on the sides of the hills but Ivor charged into them and split them like meringues.

"Keep pushing, Ivor!" shouted Jones the Steam, but Ivor needed no encouragement. His fire was burning well, his steam pressure was high. His pistons were puffing powerfully and the snow was leaping up and away on each side of them. He was enjoying himself.

It was a glorious sight. Even the sun came out to see and lit the mountains with shafts of light that glittered on the snow and ice like golden fire.

Soon they came to Grumbly Town.

Jones closed the regulator and they rolled quietly into the snow-covered station.

"Are you there Mr Thomas?" shouted Jones the Steam.

Mr Thomas, the Station-master, took his feet off the stove and put down his mug of tea.

"What's this, the Ghost Train?" he laughed. "I didn't expect to see you again till after the snow!"

"Well it's a bit of an emergency, like," explained Jones. "Eli the Baker is out of flour, Mr Davies has no potatoes and Mrs Williams is dangerously low on bull's-eyes. We can't let the town starve, can we?"

Well, it's all waiting here for you," said Mr Thomas. "I'll help you load up."

There were fifteen bags of flour, five of potatoes, nets of carrots, sprouts, onions and leeks. Boxes of bull's-eyes and beef-cubes, camphor, combs and caraway seeds, detergents and dolly-mixture, embrocation, flannel nighties, grapefruit, hatpins, hair oil, honey and so on right throught the alphabet.

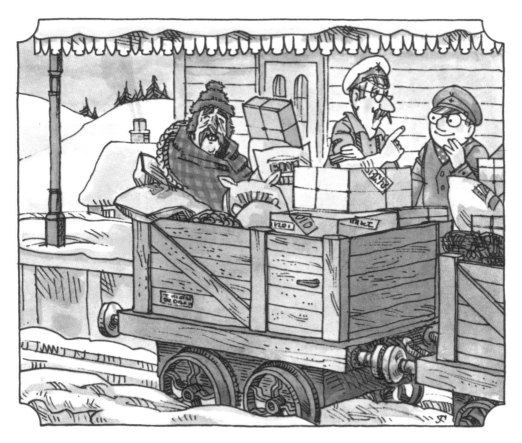

Also there was Miss Figgin's old uncle, who had come to see the dentist three weeks ago, and had had to stay ever since.

They wrapped him in blankets and packed him in with the rest of the goods.

"Mind how you go now, Ivor," said Mr Thomas. "That's a heavy load you are pulling, look, and don't bump Mr Figgin too much or he'll have to come back for a new lot of teeth!"

POOP-POOP

CHUFF CHUFF CHUFF CHUFF.

The load was very heavy but as they had cleared the line on the way down, Ivor pulled it with no trouble. They puffed merrily up the hill, through Tan-y-Gwlch and down the hill beyond the tunnel.

Then they saw trouble ahead.

Where the line went close under the hill the snow had slipped in an avalanche, and the line was blocked.

"Take a run at it, Ivor!" shouted Jones, "We've plenty of weight behind us!"

Jones opened the regulator.

POOP went Ivor's whistle as he charged joyfully at the snowpile.

SCHREECH-SLITHER...BONK-BONK...CLUNK.

Ivor had slammed on his brakes.

He stopped inches from the snowpile.

"What's wrong, Ivor?" laughed Jones. "Afraid of a bit of snow?"

They backed off and charged again.

Again, Ivor slammed on his brakes.

"Now, look here, Ivor," began Jones angrily because he had bumped his nose. "Just what do you..."

He stopped. He had seen something.

The snowpile was not all snow. Some of it looked like wool.

Jones saw a nose here, an ear and a tail there. He fetched his shovel.

"Baa," said the first sheep as he dug it out.

Jones went on digging. He dug out in all, fourteen sheep. They were very cold and miserable, but they were unharmed.

"Baa-baa-baa-baa – Baa!" they shouted.

"Yes, all right," said Jones. "but do be quiet a minute while we decide what to do with you."

There was only one thing they could do really; take the sheep to Llaniog and find out to whom they belonged.

Jones unloaded all the goods, except Miss Figgin's uncle. Then he lifted the sheep into the trucks.

"They'll be company for you, Mr Figgin."

"Baa-baa-baa," said the sheep, very pleased.

"Bah!" said Mr Figgin, very displeased.

POOP-POOP! went Ivor's whistle.

CHUFF CHUFF CHUFF.

They charged through what remained of the snowheap and headed for home.

Everybody in Llaniog was out to meet them.

"Hooray for Jones, the hero!" they shouted.

"Hooray for Ivor!"

"Have you brought my flour?" shouted Eli.

"My potatoes?" shouted Mr Davies.

"My bull's-eyes?" shouted Mrs Williams.

"Nothing but sheep!" shouted Eli angrily.

"Look! Two truckloads of sheep and if there is one thing we have plenty of in Llaniog, it is cold sheep!"

28

"Dashed impertinence!" muttered Mr Figgin.

"Where is my dolly-mixture?" wailed Mrs Williams.

POOOOOOOP went Ivor's whistle so loudly
that everybody had to stop shouting.

"Now, listen everybody," said Jones the Steam. "The goods are a mile or so back down the line. We just unload the sheep and go back for them...all right?"

They lifted down the sheep, and Mr Figgin who was still bleating.

Jones and Ivor went back down the line, and Mr Davies and Eli the Baker came too because Jones the Steam had lifted enough boxes and bags for one day.

So the sheep came home, Mr Davies got his potatoes, Mrs Williams her bull's-eyes and the next day Eli the Baker made a batch of hot fresh rolls for them all.

This edition published by Severnside Wholesalers Limited 2006

First paperback edition published by Picture Lions 1977
14 St. James's Place London SW1

First hardback edition published by Diamond Books 1994
77-85 Fulham Palace Road Hammersmith London W6 8JB

© 2006 Oliver Postgate & Peter Firmin

Printed in England by Severnprint Limited, Gloucester